Mom + Dad,
I do not mind how the
new baby is. I will
love it so so
so so so much.
X X X X
  X X

To Mom and Dad,
Can we have more so
we can have a football
team?
              Love x x X

To Mom and Dad
I am going
to give you all
big hugs.

To Mom + Dad

I will do my homework
if you don't make me
change diapers.
                    Love
                    x   x

New babies everywhere. (Welcome!)
Lee Wildish, for always adding spark,
humor, and heart. (Thank you! Thank you!)
And Jens. —J.R.

Welcome to the world, all newborns. —L.W.

THIS IS A BORZOI BOOK PUBLISHED BY ALFRED A. KNOPF

Text copyright © 2022 by Jean Reagan
Jacket art and interior illustrations copyright © 2022 by Lee Wildish

All rights reserved. Published in the United States by Alfred A. Knopf, an imprint of
Random House Children's Books, a division of Penguin Random House LLC, New York.

Knopf, Borzoi Books, and the colophon are registered trademarks of Penguin Random House LLC.

Visit us on the Web! rhcbooks.com

Educators and librarians, for a variety of teaching tools, visit us at
RHTeachersLibrarians.com

Library of Congress Cataloging-in-Publication Data is available upon request.
ISBN 978-0-593-43060-6 (trade) — ISBN 978-0-593-43061-3 (lib. bdg.) — ISBN 978-0-593-43062-0 (ebook)

The text of this book is set in 18-point Goudy Old Style.
The illustrations were created digitally.
Book design by Monique Razzouk

MANUFACTURED IN CHINA
January 2022
10 9 8 7 6 5 4 3 2 1

First Edition

How to Welcome a New Baby

BABY
COMING
SOON

BY JEAN REAGAN   ILLUSTRATED BY LEE WILDISH

ALFRED A. KNOPF 🐕 NEW YORK

A new baby is coming. Hooray! Welcoming the baby can be *your* job!

Even before the baby comes, there's a lot to do.
Your parents are busy, so remind them . . .

HOW TO GET READY FOR A BABY

Find the **perfect** name.

"Rainbow"

"Pretzel"

"T. rex"

"Buddy-Bear"

Wrap your toys for the new baby.

(Well, maybe not all of them.)

Ring

Ring

Get the baby's car seat ready.

(You're way too big now!)

Click,
click,
click.

Then, one day—the baby is here!
Now you can shout, "I'm a big
sister!" or "I'm a big brother!"

Welcome Home,
Baby

Kiss the baby and whisper, "Welcome to our family."

At first, things may be a little topsy-turvy:

"WAAAAAAA

AAAAAAAAAAAAAAAAAAA!"

Your pets might feel left out, so give them extra hugs.
If *you* need an extra hug, just ask. "Hug, please?"

Friends and family LOVE to visit brand-new babies.
You're the expert, so . . .

Warn Grandpa the baby
squeezes pinkies very,
very tightly.

Show Grandma how
your baby yawns or
hiccups. *Sometimes*
at the same time!

Remind your friends NO party food for the baby.

Make sure they know a poopy diaper means— **run away!**

When the visitors leave, you become the

Number One Helper.

HOW TO HELP WITH BABIES

If your dad gets stuck
under a sleeping baby,
bring everything he needs.

Wash their teeny-tiny toes.

Open their presents for them.

But what if the baby can't fall asleep? Share your tricks.

Whisper-sing a lullaby.

Look into the baby's eyes and say, "You are getting sleepy, you are getting sleepy, you are getting . . ."

Read your favorite
bedtime story.

Bring in reinforcements.

Once your baby can **sit up,** you might wonder, "When will this baby be ready to play with me?"

Not yet! But the baby LOVES to watch YOU, so figure out . . .

HOW TO MAKE A BABY LAUGH

Play upside-down peekaboo.

Boogie with your bear.

Find funny hats.

Blow bubbles
and chase
them till they
POP.

When your baby's learned to **stand,** it's time for a few big-kid things. Your parents know a lot, but some things only *you* can teach.

WHAT TO TEACH A BABY

Where to watch for the garbage truck.

When to stay quiet.
"Shhhhhh."

How to play train.
"All aboard!"

How to high-five.

When your baby starts to **walk,** go exploring together.

EXPLAIN HOW . . .

Ladybugs are for
counting dots.

Pine cones are
for kicking.

Leaves are for collecting.
Or crunching.

Remind your baby—none of these are for eating.

But picnics are!

CONGRATULATIONS!

You've done a super job welcoming your baby.

And one day . . .

guess who will welcome *you* home?